Ceri & Deri

THE TREASURE MAP

THIS BOOK BELONGS TO:

Llyfrgelloedd Caerdydd
www.caerdydd.gov.uk/llyfrgelloedd
Cardiff Libraries
www.cardiff.gov.uk/libraries

CAERDYDD
CARDIFF

D0178735

ACC. No: 07050904

Ceri & Deri – The Treasure Map
Published in Great Britain in 2019 by Graffeg
Limited.

Written and illustrated by Max Low,
copyright © 2019.
Designed and produced by Graffeg Limited
copyright © 2019.

Graffeg Limited, 24 Stradey Park Business Centre,
Mwrwg Road, Llangennech, Llanelli,
Carmarthenshire SA14 8YP Wales UK
Tel: 01554 824000 www.graffeg.com

Max Low is hereby identified as the author of this
work in accordance with section 77 of the
Copyrights, Designs and Patents Act 1988.

A CIP Catalogue record for this book is available
from the British Library.

All rights reserved. No part of this publication
may be reproduced, stored in a retrieval system
or transmitted, in any form or by any means,
electronic, mechanical, photocopying, recording
or otherwise, without the prior permission of the
publishers.

ISBN 9781912213764

1 2 3 4 5 6 7 8 9

Ceri & Deri

THE TREASURE MAP

Max Low

Ceri

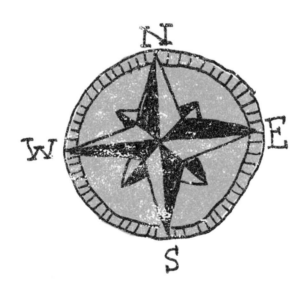

Deri

GRAFFEG

Ceri is a cat and Deri is a dog.

Ceri has stripes and Deri has spots.

They live in a small town near a big hill and they do everything together.

They are best friends.

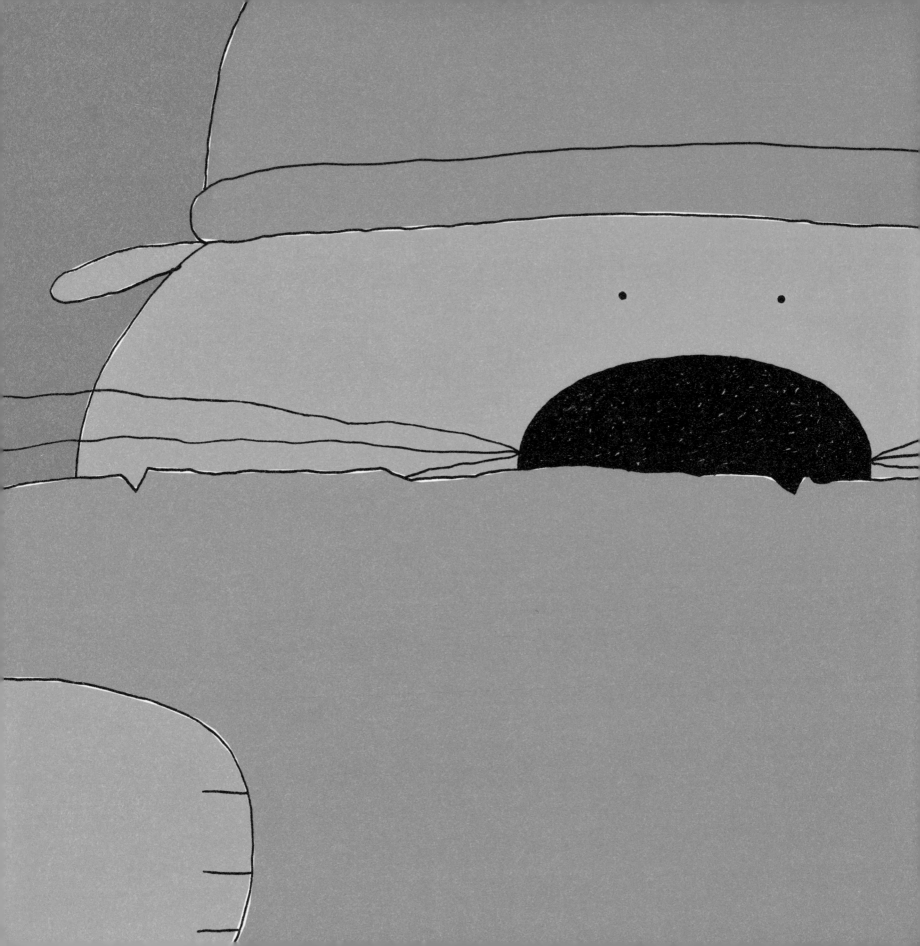

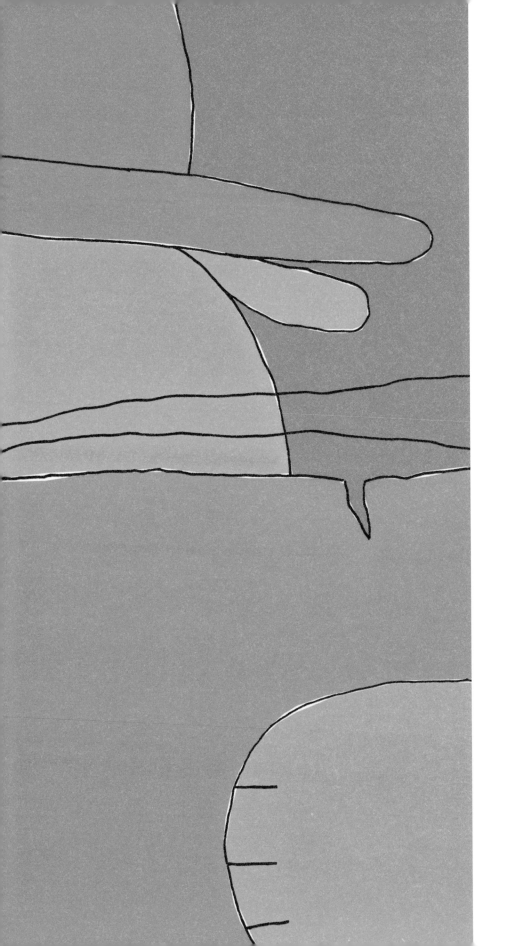

On an otherwise very ordinary day, Ceri has brought along a map...

It is a map, but not just any map...

A TREASURE map!

'Where did you get that old map from?' asks Deri.

'My nan's nan, she was a pirate...it's a treasure map!' says Ceri, as they both look at the old parchment.

'OOOOOH!' says Deri, who likes maps and pirates and treasure almost as much as cake.

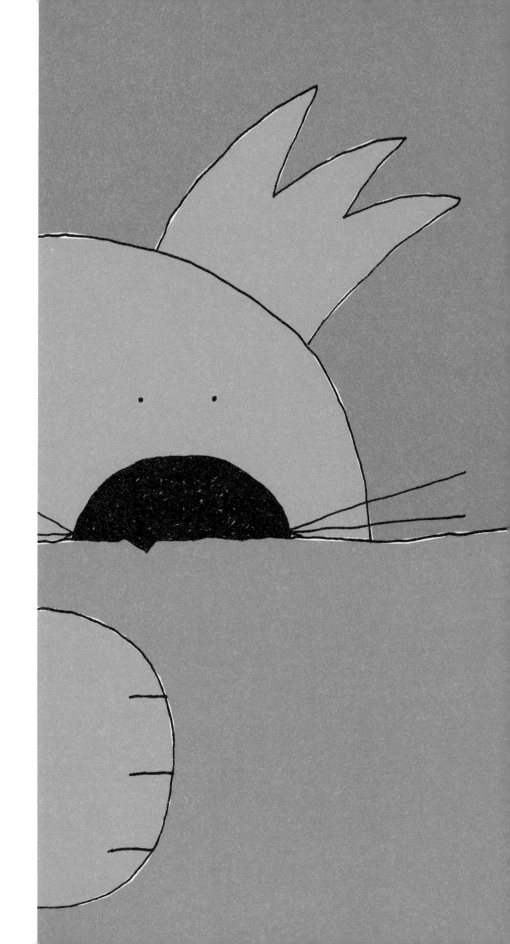

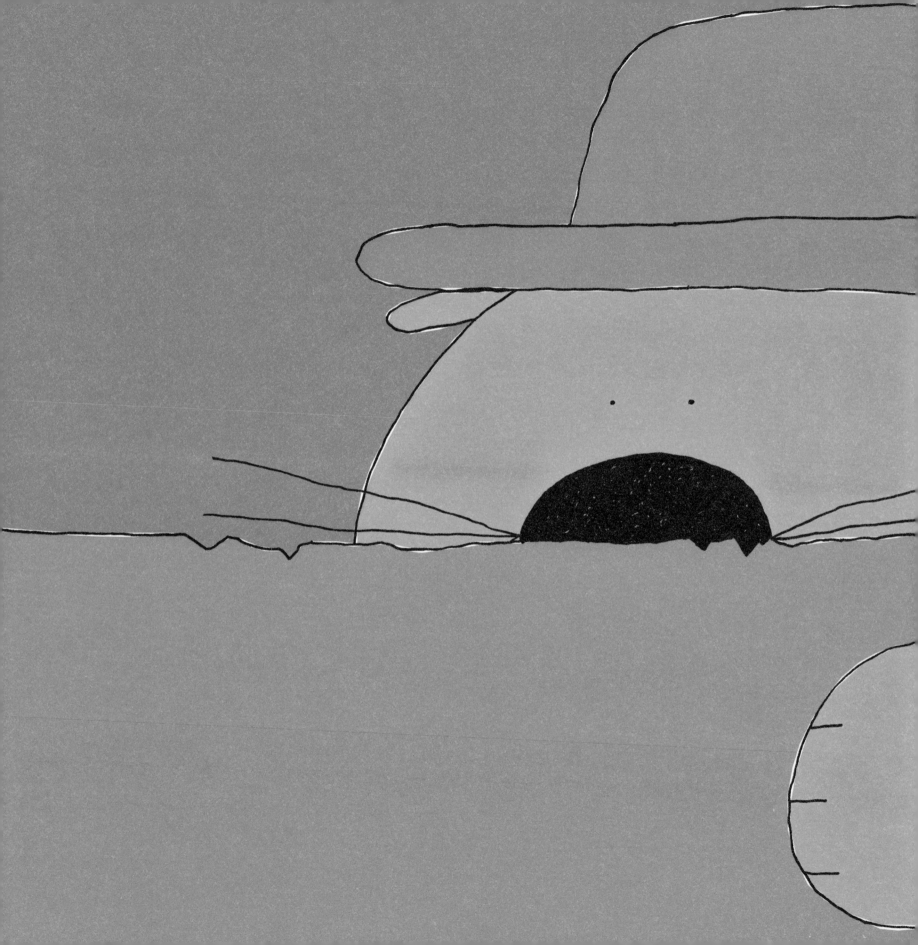

'She sailed all around the world on the high seas, swashbuckling and buckswashling!' explains Ceri.

'Wow! I wish I was a pirate!' says Deri.

'Well, let's go and find this treasure then!' says Ceri.

'Aye, aye, Cap'n!' says Deri.

The map is so old and pirate-like that Ceri and Deri can't help but shake with excitement.

'Look! The treasure is buried on the beach, of all places!' says Ceri.

'The beach! What an odd place to bury treasure!' says Deri.

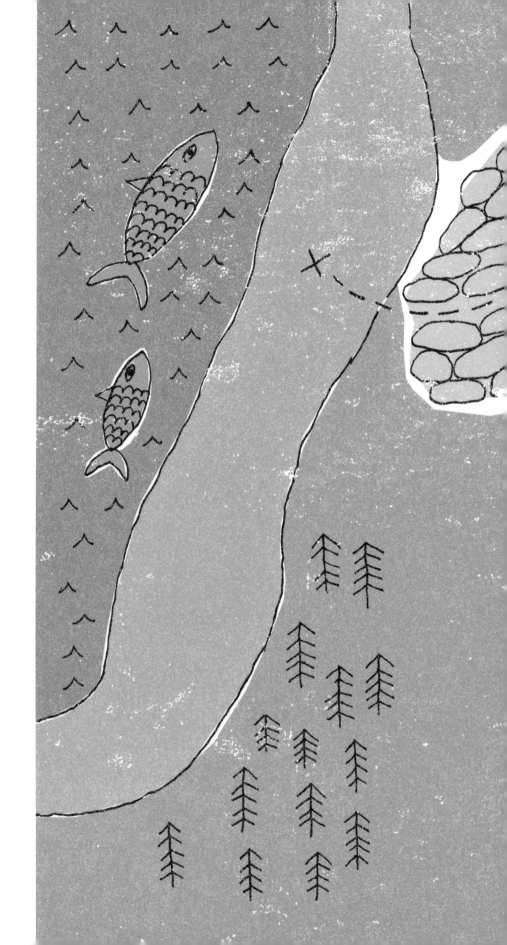

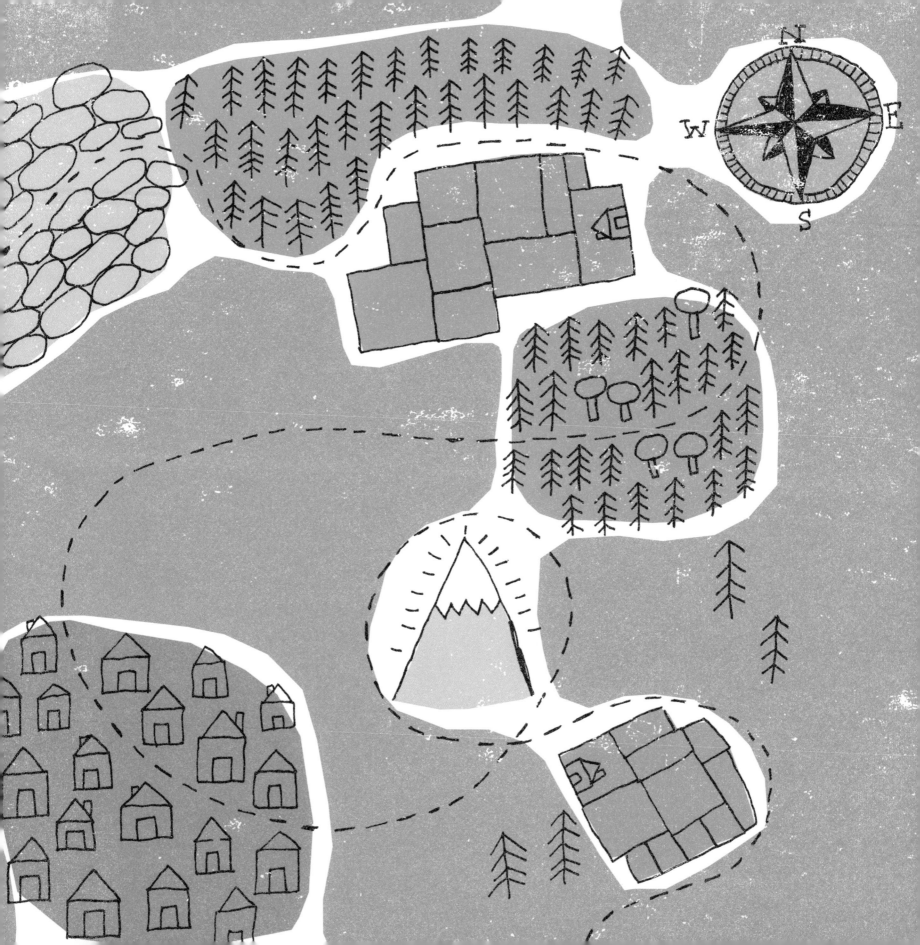

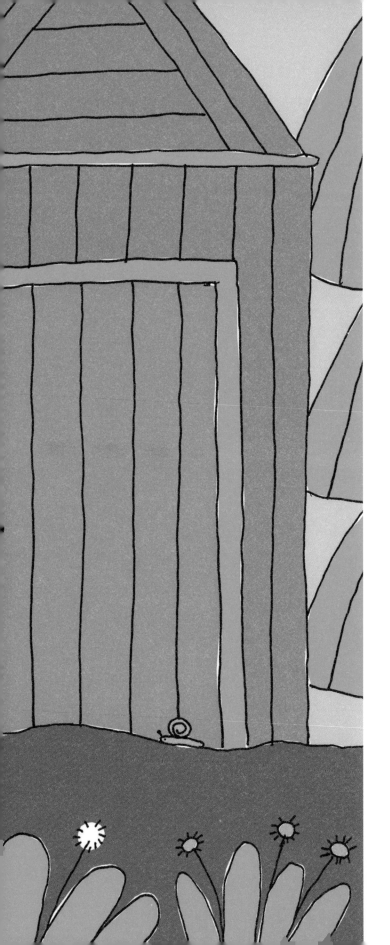

They set out on their adventure and follow the treasure map to their right. It leads them first to the allotment, where all the dandelions and snails are.

'Where are you two troublemakers off to?' asks Gardener Glesni.

'We are looking for buried treasure!' says Ceri.

'OOH, can I come with you?' asks Gardener Glesni, who likes maps and pirates and treasure almost as much as dandelions and snails.

'Of course! Let's go!' says Deri.

They follow the treasure map to their left as it leads them up a steep hill.

It's hard work, but it also means they can go...

...down the steep hill, which isn't hard work at all.

As the three gather their breath after all that exercise, the treasure map leads them to their right and past Owain's Opticians, with its rows and rows of stylish spectacles.

'Where are you three troublemakers off to?' asks Optician Owain.

'We are looking for buried treasure!' says Ceri.

'OOH, can I come with you?' asks Optician Owain, who likes maps and pirates and treasure almost as much as stylish spectacles.

'Of course! Let's go!' says Deri.

With Ceri in the lead, the four follow the treasure map straight ahead, deep into the forest.

There is so much green!

They go left and right through the trees and invent a path around the trunks as they go.

The map finally guides them to their left and through Ffion's farm, where there are vegetables and mud.

'Where are you four troublemakers off to?' asks Farmer Ffion.

'We are looking for buried treasure!' says Ceri.

'OOH, can I come with you?' asks farmer Ffion, who likes maps and pirates and treasure almost as much as vegetables and mud.

'Of course! Let's go!' says Deri.

The five soon leave the farm behind and follow the treasure map to their right and then straight on.

They have to watch their step across big rocks and blue and grey boulders.

They must be near the sea now, they can smell it!

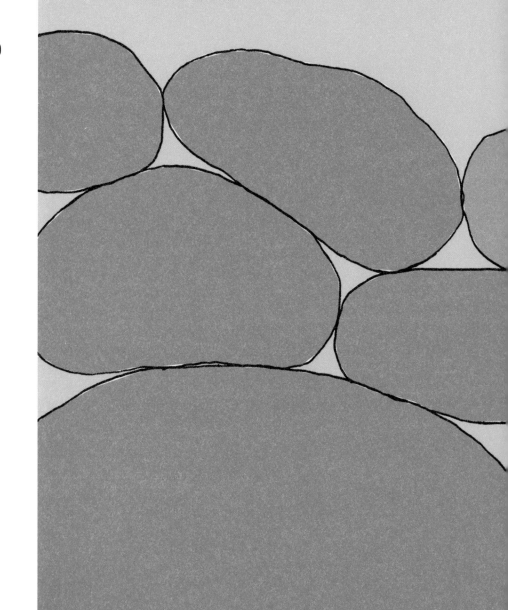

And there it is, right ahead of them...

The sea!

It is calm and shimmering blue as far as their eyes can see.

They go down to the sandy beach and Ceri and Deri begin digging excitedly, right where the X tells them.

'Of all the places to bury treasure!' says Gardener Glesni.

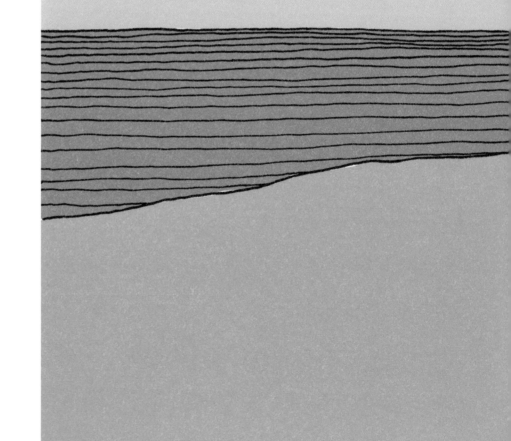

'I've found something!' says Ceri.

Everyone helps her to dig the thing up.

'It's a treasure chest!' Ceri says.

They can barely contain themselves at the discovery and Optician Owain starts to hop up and down with excitement.

'What's inside it?' he asks.

Ceri slowly lifts the old, old lid...

PIRATE COSTUMES!

The gang try on the costumes and soon they all look the part. Now they feel ready for many more pirate-y adventures!

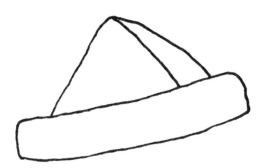

'Hey Deri, what did the ocean say to the pirates?' asks Ceri.

'I don't know, Ceri, what did the ocean say to the pirates?' says Deri.

'Nothing, it just waved.'

Ceri & Deri

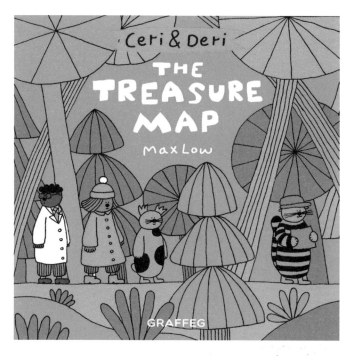

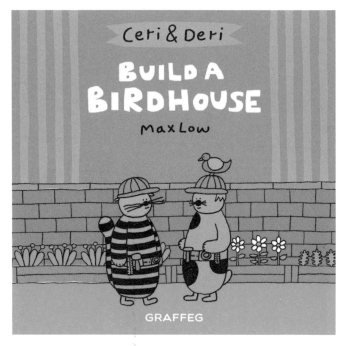